The Glass Bottle Tree

by

Evelyn Coleman

illustrated by

Gail Gordon Carter

ORCHARD BOOKS

New York

*To my grandmother, the late
Mary Saunders; my daughters,
Travara and Latrayan; and all the
children who grow up with
unconditional love in
nontraditional families*
—E.C.

*In memory of Leona, Bertha, and Dora;
to grandmothers and grandmother
figures everywhere*
—G.G.C.

Orchard Books
95 Madison Avenue
New York, NY 10016

Manufactured in the United States of America
Printed by Barton Press, Inc.
Bound by Horowitz/Rae
Book design by Rosanne Kakos-Main
10 9 8 7 6 5 4 3 2 1

The text of this book is set in 18 point Adobe Caslon.
The illustrations are watercolor and colored pencil on watercolor paper.

Library of Congress Cataloging-in-Publication Data

Coleman, Evelyn, date.
The glass bottle tree / by Evelyn Coleman; illustrated by Gail Gordon Carter.
p.   cm.
Summary: Living together way out in the country, an African American girl and her
grandmother have such a close relationship that they communicate without words.
ISBN 0-531-09467-7. --ISBN 0-531-08767-0 (lib. bdg.)
[1. Afro-Americans--Fiction. 2. Grandmothers--Fiction.]
I. Carter, Gail Gordon, ill. II. Title.
PZ7.C6746G1 1995
[E]--dc20   94-45921

Author's Note

As a child, while riding in a car in the deep South, I saw a tree with colorful bottles stuck on its limbs. My grandmother told me the bottles were there to hold the spirits of our ancestors, an African-American belief spirited all the way from Africa. I fashioned my own glass bottle tree when I got home so that I could talk to my ancestors.

The practice of creating glass bottle trees has diminished with time. However, Julie Dash displays a glass bottle tree in her movie *Daughters of the Dust*. I hope that even today you might be lucky enough to see one while traveling dusty roads in the deep South. Or maybe you'll make your own, as I did, in order to talk to your ancestors.

Once upon a summer's breeze, way, way down in the country, a little girl lived peacefully with her grandmother. They lived in a rickety old house, with a makeshift pickety fence, down a long, long dusty road. And smack-dab in the middle of their yard was an old tree.

This was no ordinary tree, for the old grandmother believed spirits lived in it. Old spirits from far away and near, spirits with good thoughts, some with mistaken thoughts, and spirits that seemed like they had no thoughts at all, but all spirits of the family.

Sometimes those old spirits would get to laughing and arguing and telling stories to the little girl, until they'd get so riled they'd stir up the wind. Everything in the grandmother's yard would then become a whirling, swirling mess of kin.

And so one day the grandmother decided to put all the spirits inside bottles, so they'd get ahold of themselves and behave. She took her granddaughter by the hand and showed her how to place the bottles on the limbs of the old tree, like her grandmother had done before her. Grandmothers know how to keep spirits quiet.

Then she and the little girl went about their daily business. But not before the grandmother noticed the reeds in the fields bending low to the ground and the grasshoppers singing their warning song. She knew a terrible storm was brewing, even if there wasn't one cloud in the sky. Yessiree, trouble was on the way.

Early in the mornings, with a thud of a hoe and the twill of a tiller and the drop of a seed and the rhythmic bending of knees, it wasn't long before the grandmother taught the little girl how to make vegetables and flowers sprout up to reach for the sun, without saying one word to her.

In the evenings, at the banks of the river, with a
dip and a bob and a swishing of arms and a kicking of
legs, the grandmother soon taught the little girl to
swim, without the swish of a sound, alongside the
rainbow-colored brim.

After supper, sitting in front of an evening fire, with the twist of wrists, the fold of fingers, and the clicking of four long needles through colorful yarns, the grandmother taught the little girl to knit a winter blanket, without speaking one single solitary word.

On Sundays, with butterflies on their shoulders, blue jays eating from their hands, bees whispering near their ears, and animals snuggled close, the grandmother taught the little girl to enjoy a simple picnic, without either of them opening their mouths.

And every night, before bed, they silently told each other good-night. In the stillness, they waited for the cricket's lullaby to put them to sleep.

The grandmother and the little girl were very happy until the day some folk who worked for the state came. They came to discuss the little girl who lived in the rickety old house with the pickety fence down the long, long dusty road.

After visiting with the little girl and her grandmother and observing neither of them being much for talking, the state's folk reasoned that the little girl would be much better off living with a well-to-do family in a beautiful yuppety house. One where there was a mother and father and two children who all talked to one another a lot.

There would definitely be no pet mouse or chickens or any goats lingering about. And above all no weird tree growing in the yard with silly glass bottles stuck all over it.

"The grandmother's too old to keep the little girl," the one said. "Why, she's so old she can't see good."

"She can't hear good either," said the other.

"And it seems like she might not be able to talk. She never says a word," said the first. "I'm sure the little girl will feel better in a real family."

So they decided.

They hadn't noticed the things the grandmother taught the little girl to see, and hear, and do. They hadn't heard the talk the grandmother taught the little girl to talk without using her voice. And they sure never recognized the love the grandmother and the little girl shared.

So in the fall's breeze, the folk who worked for the state returned. They came down the long, long, now muddy road. And this time they came for the little girl.

The grandmother sat on her old rickety porch, rocking in her chair. "Trouble done come." She sighed. But she kept right on rocking even after they bundled the little girl up and stepped off into the muddy yard.

The grandmother never once lifted her eyes, nor opened her ears, nor said one single solitary word. She only felt great sadness as she heard her granddaughter crying. So she spoke to the spirits in the tree. She spoke to them with a ritual of rocking and humming, rocking and humming, and rocking and humming some more, a ritual her grandmother had taught her long ago.

Well, the state's folk, convinced by the grandmother's strange behavior that they were doing the right thing, were about to wave good-bye to the grandmother when the animals, that old tree, and the spirits of the family heard the little girl's crying, and the grandmother's rocking, humming, and pining.

But the state's folk couldn't hear the grandmother. They were just standing there frowning in disgust at her rocking in that chair so wildly. Suddenly the spirits in that old tree and its bottles started swaying back and forth, back and forth, and back and forth some more. Those bottles started jiggling and jaggling, clinking and clanking, and wiggling and waggling like they were go'n jump right off the tree. And they did.

Then the wind began howling, and the spirits that had been held inside the glass bottles commenced to prowling. The spirits jumped from one person to another and flung those state's folk here and there and everywhere.

By the time everything had settled down and the last tinkle had tinkled, the state's folk were lying outside the rickety old fence, like worn-out rag dolls.

"Well, well," one spoke up in a tiny voice. "I believe that old woman has the best eyesight I've ever seen."

"Me too, me too," said the other. "Why, she can hear better than any person I know."

"You're right. You're right," said the first, trembling so badly his knees knocked together. "And she always knows just the right thing to say."

Indeed she did. The old woman hobbled down off the porch and waved good-bye.

After that, she picked up the little girl and looked into her eyes, and told her, "I love you."

The little girl answered back, "I love you too, Grandmother."

Neither of them had opened their mouths.

And the glass bottle tree didn't open its mouth either, because the grandmother began putting the bottles back, before the spirits could get all riled up, gossiping about their latest adventure. As the grandmother watched the little girl place the last bottle back on the tree, she wore a big smile. She knew the little girl had learned one more thing about her family.

And as the state's folk headed down the long, long country road, they agreed between themselves never to come back for the little girl again, without either of them opening their mouths.